How Does Sleep Come?

JEANNE C. BLACKMORE

PICTURES BY ELIZABETH SAYLES

sourcebooks
jabberwocky

"How does sleep come?" Jacob asked
his mama as he climbed into bed.
Jacob's mama tucked the covers all
around Jacob just so, and then she told him.

"Sleep comes quietly.
Like a snowfall that blankets a
meadow on a dark starry night
and lays down a soft white canvas
for rabbits to leave footprints."

Jacob snuggled under his covers.

"Sleep comes silently.
Like a fog that rolls into a harbor
and shrouds the boats in misty gray,
making a silence broken only by
the clang of buoys."

Jacob yawned and stretched.

"Sleep comes softly.
Like a cloud that drifts through
a bright summer sky and
sweeps a cool shadow across the land."

Jacob sighed and curled up.

"Sleep comes peacefully.
Like a cat that curls up cozily
in front of a warm fire,
and kneads its paws as it purrs."

Jacob's eyelids grew heavy.

"Sleep comes gently.
Like a butterfly that lands
delicately on your hand
and slowly brings its wings to rest."

Jacob closed his eyes.

And the snow fell.
And the fog rolled in.
And the clouds drifted.

And the cat purred.
And the butterfly alit.

And quietly, silently, softly,
peacefully, gently,

Jacob fell asleep.

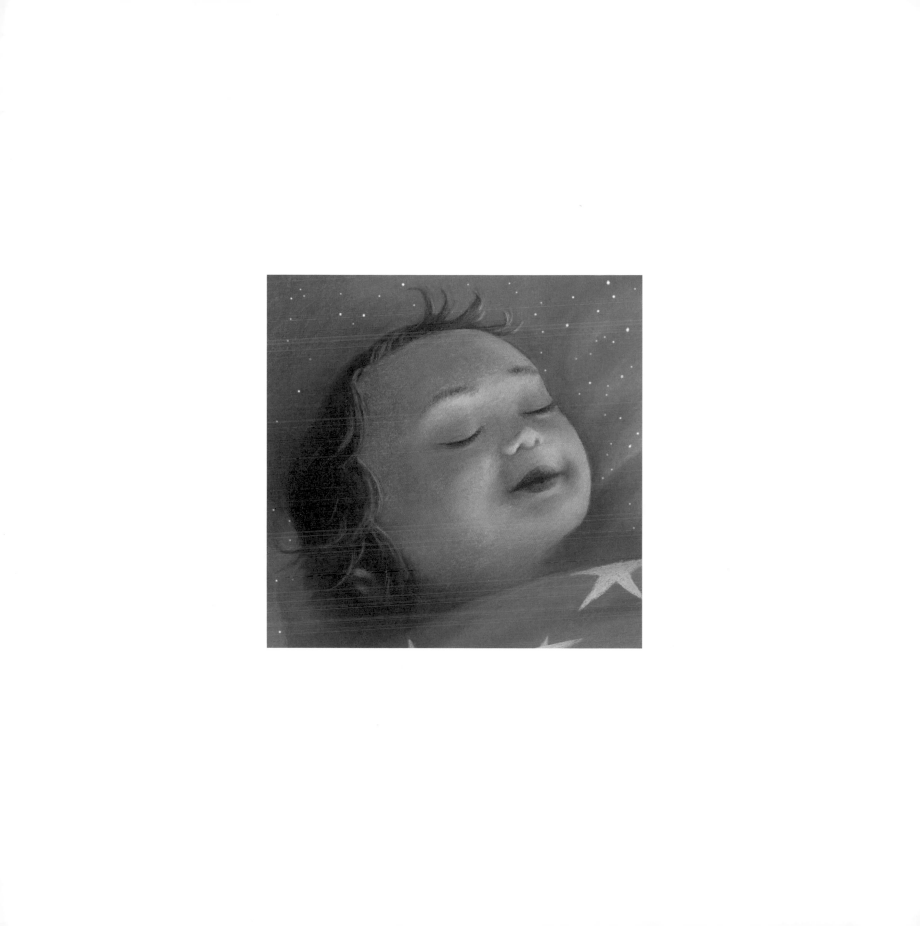

To Ben and Sammie,
and to Jacob Byrnes, the first baby of the bunch

Jeanne C. Blackmore works as an attorney during the day and, unable to resist the storytelling heritage of her family, writes in her spare time. Jeanne's grandfather, Roger Duvoisin, was a well-known children's book author and illustrator, and all of her siblings are authors of one sort or another. Jeanne lives in northern Vermont with her husband and their two children, along with two dogs, several chickens, and a bunch of hermit crabs.

Elizabeth Sayles has illustrated more than twenty-five books for children including the *New York Times* #1 bestselling picture book, *I Already Know I Love You* by Billy Crystal. She is adjunct professor of Illustration at the School of Visual Arts in New York City. She lives in the lower Hudson Valley of New York with her husband and their daughter.

Published by Sourcebooks Jabberwocky, an imprint of Sourcebooks, Inc.
P.O. Box 4410, Naperville, Illinois 60567-4410
(630) 961-3900
Fax: (630) 961-2168
www.jabberwockykids.com

Library of Congress Cataloging-in-Publication data is on file with the publisher.

Source of Production: Bang Printing, Brainerd, Minnesota, USA
Date of Production: July 2012
Run Number: 18101

Printed and bound in the United States of America.
BG 10 9 8 7 6 5 4 3 2 1